The Problem with Humans

And Other Stories

Allison Spooner

A Dish Best Served Canned

"I'm not sure we should be doing this," Liza said.

"Of course we should." David was rummaging through a bag and barely looked up. "The old broad's got more money than she knows what to do with and this guy is offering us some real change for the thing."

"But, she's pretty attached to it."

"So? I was pretty attached to my job. Besides, the thing is hideous. We're doing her a favor." Liza sighed. "I guess, but …"

"Look, she fired me for no reason. She's old and ornery and she deserves this. It'll be easy, I promise."

Upstairs, Mrs. Black was already in bed.

"I'm sorry about your friend," she said as Liza drew the curtains and tidied up around the bedroom. Liza didn't respond. The old woman had treated Liza like a daughter since she'd shown up five years ago with no family, looking for work. But David had become her family over the last few years and it was going to take more than an apology for Liza to forgive Mrs. Black for letting him go. David was right. She did deserve what they were about to do.

David gently closed Liza's fingers around the metal.

"You know what to do, right?"

"I'll wait until she's asleep …"

David nodded.

"And then I take this back into the bedroom."

He nodded again, eagerly.

"From there," he said, "It'll be simple."

"Simple," she repeated, her voice barely a whisper.

"Liza." David's voice was stern. "She doesn't care about you. You're just an employee. She can act as sweet as she wants, but that's how she thinks about you."

"Liza, turn around please." Liza stopped her straightening and turned to face the woman in the bed. White and pink pillows surrounded her and with the shock of white curls framing her face, she could have been floating on a cloud. Liza had laid in the bed once, when Mrs. Black was out of town. It certainly felt like a cloud.

"Dear, I know you and Mr. Ash were close …" Liza was surprised she knew his last name. "But you're better off putting some distance there, trust me."

Liza turned her head to avoid eye contact and saw it. Next to Mrs. Black on the bed. She looked away. It really *was* hideous.

"She'll do to you what she did to me," David pressed. "Trust me. It's only a matter of time."

Liza looked down. It was hard to imagine Mrs. Black suddenly letting her go; she didn't really have anyone else in that big house with her. Except for Frances.

"Hey." David took her chin between his thumb and forefinger. "We do this, and we can get a train ticket out of here. With the money we get from selling it, we can be a family."

She nodded.

"Oh," he said, reaching back into the bag. "Don't forget this." He leaned forward, offering what he had pulled out of the bag. "You'll need this."

The metal was cool in her hand.

"You know I think of you as family, dear. Young love can be powerful, but there are things you don't know about your young man."

Liza looked down to the floor as the thing beside Mrs. Black stirred and shifted. The two objects in her dress pockets weighed heavy against her.

"Mr. Ash was stealing from me."

Liza's head jerked up.

"I know it's a shock, but it's true." She reached over and pulled the thing closer, as though protecting it. Liza's hand hovered over her pockets.

"The mechanic found him in the garage. Apparently, he was taking parts from my dear-departed-Richard's rare cars and selling them."

"Car parts?" Liza whispered.

"She owes us, Liza. We can barely afford to support ourselves. We live like servants!" He motioned around them. The place *was* a bit of a dump. The paint was peeling, the sinks never stopped dripping and David said anything that couldn't fit in the garage he was told to put down here, including boxes of old car parts and tools. "And now, firing me for no reason?" He scoffed. "Do you know how much she probably paid for that thing? It's ridiculous. And it's so goddam ugly. Once we take it, she can spring for a cat with hair."

The hairless cat stretched out beside Mrs. Black as she nodded. "Apparently, it's been going on for quite some time. He probably made a fortune." Liza thought of the boxes of parts piled in the corners of their quarters and felt sick. He'd lied. "The money isn't important to me, of course, but those cars meant the world to Richard. I was going to donate them to his favorite charity so they could auction them off, but now…" Mrs. Black shook her head and looked down at Frances, its great bug eyes gazing up lovingly at her. "We just had to dismiss him. Right, Frances?"

She really loved that damn cat. Liza wondered if David even had a buyer lined up for Frances or if he only wanted revenge.

4

"Thank you for telling me," Liza said, approaching the bed. She touched the woman's hand, "Goodnight, Mrs. Black."

"Goodnight, dear."

Liza reached over and patted the top of Frances's head. His skin was leathery and she had to hold back a shiver. "Goodnight, Frances."

Liza stood outside Mrs. Black's door, waiting. When she heard the gentle sounds of snoring, she took the can opener from one pocket and the can of cat food from the other and put them in the box meant for Frances. She quietly entered the bedroom. Tiptoeing to the dresser, she lifted the lid of Mrs. Black's jewelry box and pulled out a glittery glob of jewels. To an amateur eye, to someone looking to make a quick buck stealing from an old woman, they would look expensive, but Liza knew they were only trinkets. The box full, she went to the door. She looked back at the bed and saw Frances glaring at her as though the cat knew the fate it had just escaped. Liza gave her a quick wink before slipping out the door. Fucking ugly cat.

After she'd slipped downstairs and deposited the box in David's room next to the confirmed stolen car parts, Liza went into the parlor, where she phoned the police. "Yes, I'd like to report a crime at the Black Estate ... theft and attempted cat-napping."

The Flight

She didn't realize she was allergic to cigarette smoke until she took a job at the smoking lounge in the airport. Now, she spent all her time fixing drinks, wiping at her watering eyes, and cursing the tobacco companies. Well, that and staring out the glass window to the rest of the airport waiting for him to walk by.

Him.

The too-handsome-for-words pilot walked by several times a week on his way to one exotic destination after another. Cities like Bali, Tahiti, or … Phoenix. Places she could only dream of going. The ridiculously tanned, toned, and lean athlete who would probably never sacrifice his respiratory health by setting foot in an airport smoking lounge.

She glanced at the clock. He hadn't passed yet today and would probably be going by any … any … *achoo*! Ugh. Damn this smoke. She glared at the one oblivious patron at the end of the bar as she reached for a cocktail napkin and swiped at her dripping nose. Who still smoked, anyway? Didn't he know it would kill him? Maybe if it did, she would get to go home early and just never come back. And try to find a job that wasn't slowly killing her.

She blew her nose into the napkin, not even bothering trying to hide it from him. Let him be as grossed out by her snot as she was by his disgusting habit. Still wiping her nose, she looked up to the window and there he was. Just standing. Not walking, not hurrying, but standing and staring. At her? Couldn't be. She looked behind her but the man at the bar didn't seem to know Handsome Pilot. He was definitely looking at her. Cocktail napkin still pressed to her nose, she watched in horror as he stepped through the glass doors and into the lounge.

He approached the bar. "Are you okay?"

She threw the napkin behind her. "Uhh …" Before she could respond with actual words, he reached down into the front pocket of his suitcase and pulled out a bandana.

"Here, it's the closest thing I have to a handkerchief." A handkerchief. He was adorable.

"Thanks," she whispered and dabbed at her eyes with the cloth. There was no way she was blowing her nose on anything this man might put anywhere on his body.

"I couldn't just walk by a crying woman without stopping to see if she was okay." He was a goddamned gentleman.

"That's sweet." She was still whispering.

He tipped his head to the side as though he were studying her, his blue eyes meeting hers and not letting go. "*You* seem sweet. Too sweet to be working in an airport smoking lounge."

She giggled. Yes, actually giggled. Was he real?

Still not taking his eyes from hers, he let go of his suitcase and leaned across the bar, motioning with a crook of his finger for her to do the same. She looked around. Was she being punk'd? Her breath stuck her throat, she placed her forearms on the bar and leaned her face toward his. Now their noses were only inches apart.

"Would you like to go somewhere with me?" he whispered, his hot breath reaching her lips and causing her to shiver. It smelled like spearmint.

"Somewhere?" she squeaked.

"Anywhere. Let's just get on a plane and go somewhere warm. All you'll need is a bathing suit. I'll buy the Mai Tais." She just stared, too stunned to respond. "Oh yeah," he said, leaning even closer, until his lips were practically pressed against her ear. "I don't smoke."

Sold. She nodded. "Okay."

He reached out a hand. She took it and let him lead her around the bar, out into the lounge, as the smoker down the way looked up to see why there wasn't a fresh drink in front of him. Pulling off the black apron they insisted she wear, she threw it on the floor and raised her hand in farewell to her one customer. Hand in hand, they stepped through the glass door, ready to take flight together.

"Hello? Excuse me, are you sure you're okay?"

She blinked. She was back behind the bar. Handsome Pilot was standing in front of her and the smoking man was ready for another drink.

She looked down. She was still holding her hand around the bandana he was trying to give her, her fingers resting against his soft wrist.

"Where did you go there?" he asked.

Away with you, she thought. "I'm sorry," she said.

He laughed. "Don't be sorry …" he trailed off and looked to her nametag. "Liz."

She smiled at the sound of her name on his lips.

"Well, hey. I hope you're okay now. I have to catch a 7:00 to Austin. It was nice to meet you."

He's lying, she thought. All she'd done was stare at him and now he was leaving. No plane, no Mai Tais, no glorious future filled with tiny, adorable, pilot babies.

He turned toward the doors and she sighed at his retreating figure, ready to go back to admiring him from afar. She looked down at the bandana still clutched in her hand, wondering if it smelled like him. Before she could press it to her nose, she heard her name.

"Hey, Liz?"

She lifted her head. He was in the doorway, looking back at her.

"Can I stop back by tomorrow and see you?"

She nodded. *Hell yes,* she thought. "Sure," she said.

Lester The Lugubrious

"My name is Lester the Lugubrious and I'm a villain."

"Hi, Lester."

"The problem is ... I'm not a very good villain. I…" He shifted his gaze to the table stocked with coffee and doughnuts rather than make eye contact with the other members of the circle. "I don't really like it."

A murmur rolled through the group and Lester was taken back to the moment he'd had this same conversation with his father.

"Disgraceful," he'd snarled, twirling his black mustache with one hand. The conversation had landed him here, the Center for Faulty or Malfunctioning Villains. The others in the group had simply screwed up in the course of their villain duties; apparently, he was the first to want to shun them altogether.

The director, a tall thin woman with jet black hair and a tight leather corset who kept glancing at her watch, spoke above the eruption of voices. "When did you begin to notice these feelings, Lester?"

"I think I've always felt like this. When I was five, there was a cat stuck in a tree in our yard and ... I rescued it."

There was a collective gasp and this time even the director couldn't hide the disdain that so closely mimicked his father's.

"You come from a long line of villains," his father spat, pacing the kitchen. "We have worked for decades to spread fear and strike terror into the hearts of children. We have fought the strongest of heroes!"

"And we have always lost!"

"You watch your mouth."

"I'm tired of fighting," Lester continued to the group. They were really uncomfortable now, looking to each other for support, to the director to make him stop. "I want to *help* people."

"We do help!" exclaimed a man with a long scar across his face. He approached Lester until their noses almost touched. "You can't have heroes without evil to fight."

Lester shrugged. He didn't care. He just wanted to save people.

Then, from somewhere outside, an explosion rang out, shaking their building. The floor vibrated. Dust fell from the ceiling.

A crack from above made Lester look up just as a beam directly above their heads worked its way loose. Without thinking, Lester outstretched his arms, pushing the man with the scar out of the way. The beam met Lester's head instead.

When the world came back to him, he knew it wouldn't be for long. He felt himself drifting away but stopped when he heard his name. The man with the scarred face was leaning over him, he seemed to be saying the same thing over and over. "You saved me, Lester! Thank you. You saved me!"

Lester smiled.

All That Was Left

The fog was thick that morning as Lana made her way to the church. It began as a slight haze but slowly thickened as the moments ticked by, gradually dimming the rising sun. It was strange, she thought, nearing the church, usually fog *dissipated* when the sun gained strength. But today was an unusual day in itself. A day for goodbyes, for moving on, for letting go.

Everyone was already in the church when she reached the doors but, unlike every other day, she knew her mother wouldn't chide her for being late, not today. Even the last time they'd talked, she'd pleaded with her only daughter to just be on time for once in her life. Today though, Lana wanted to be late. She wanted to slow down. But there was no delaying the inevitable.

When she entered the church, the fog seemed to creep in behind her, rolling across the marble floor, pawing at her feet like a kitten.

The vestibule was empty and organ music was already pushing its way out into the hall. She noticed, before joining the mourners in the sanctuary, that the mirror on the wall beside her was covered with a sheet. A Welsh death tradition her family still honored when a loved one passed.

She made her way down the center aisle, eyeing the pews filled with friends, family, neighbors...but she didn't pause her progress toward the open casket. A small favor, she'd heard her mother say just after the accident, that we can see her beautiful face one more time.

Her mother sat in the front row, quietly sobbing into her handkerchief. The same one she'd tried to give Lana on her eighteenth birthday but she'd refused because who used handkerchiefs anymore? She also wore pearls, because, she said, every woman should own a nice pair of pearls. More than likely, she smelled like lavender, but Lana's senses were already too dull to know for sure. The rest of the church, all the mourners, were enveloped by the fog that had followed her down the aisle. She didn't have much time.

"I told her not to be late," her mother whispered to her aunt through her tears. "She was rushing because of me."

"It's okay, Mom." Lana tried to speak but the fog stole her voice. "It's not your fault." She tried to reach out to her mother, but the black dress faded, the bright pearls dulled, the handkerchief disappeared.

"Mom…" Lana whispered. The words came out as a breeze and tickled her mother's hair. The older woman gasped and then the fog pulled her away. All that was left was goodbye.

The Guardians of Willow

Long ago, a child came to the trees.

Born of war, this child was brought into the world through the union of a great warrior king and his kidnapped bride. While his wife was a treasured prize from one of his many victorious battles, the child was merely an inconvenient product of the spoils of war, and was treated as such. Ignored by the war-hungry king, shunned by the reluctant and home-sick queen, as soon as she could walk, she turned her back on the castle that was never truly her home.

Not far from the grounds, before the edge of the surrounding village, stood a quiet wood filled with strong, solid trees of every kind. The small, frightened child fell gratefully into their outstretched arms, stumbling onto the soft moss of their shade before she could even talk. They comforted her with their whispers.

As the cocoa-haired child grew, the trees became her solace. Unwanted and unloved by those meant to care for her, she found solace under their arms and played in the dangling, dancing branches that softly kissed her cheeks.

Ruled by a king who lived for battle, the castle pulsed with a violent energy, but the trees radiated gentleness. The walls of the palace vibrated with the war cries of soldiers and the lessons learned from battle; the trees taught her peace. They buzzed with energy. What she knew of life, she learned from them. They did harm to no one, and offered the breath of life to all who surrounded them.

In the castle, she would have been offered as a prize, forced to marry into a conquered kingdom, a pawn in the violent game her father had mastered. She chose not to return to the castle. The trees became her home, their moss her bed, their language her own, their whispers her lullabies. Their thoughts were hers and the more time she spent with them, the more attuned she became to their feelings. She knew nothing of humans, only the peace of the trees.

It soon became known across the kingdom that the only child of the king and queen had spurned them, turned to the wild, and become a feral beast. To many, she was simply a rumor, but it was often said that, on the days the army rode off to war, she could be seen chasing after them, pleading with them to reconsider each battle and practice peace within the kingdom. "What a shame," the townsfolk whispered, "that the child of such a great warrior should be ashamed of his conquests." It was soon decreed by an insulted and embarrassed king that anyone coming across the princess was forbidden to make contact with her. She was to be treated as the trees and flowers of the woods she loved so much—observed but not given a greeting, a polite exchange, or even an extra thought.

The trees accepted her as one of their own and to them she became known as Willow. And there, in the shade of their arms, Willow lived peacefully as a part of the woods until she was fifteen.

Then, when the child was on the verge of becoming a woman, the outside world crossed into her sanctuary and the peace of Willow's existence was disturbed by a fluttering in her chest. The man that crossed into her shady cove took her breath away. Her heart danced like the branches of her guardians when he smiled in surprise at finding her there.

"You are the princess of this kingdom, I presume?" He bowed in greeting and the heart that knew nothing of humans was suddenly lost to one. "You may call me Andreas."

When Andreas looked at her, he did not see just another tree or flower, he saw nature itself. Her shining hair was the color of the acorns littering the forest floor and her eyes matched the leaves falling around him. Her skin was touched by the sun and her cheeks were rosy with energy and life. He disregarded the decree that she should be ignored and their love washed over them like a sudden storm.

But as the rush of their romance roared in her ears, the trees fell silent. Caught up in their courtship, many days passed before Willow noticed the absence of their whispers. Still more days fell away before she tried to rouse them. While she was deeply in love, she began to miss the comfort of her first family. She wanted to share the beauty of her life with her dear one, but as long as the trees stayed silent, she could not.

At first, her efforts were futile. With Andreas by her side, she called to them. But, no matter how she tried, the only sounds that came back to her were the occasional bird song from deeper in the wood. Andreas only smiled sadly and stroked her hair and she knew he couldn't see the trees for what they were.

"Worry not, my love. You are miracle enough for me."

Because of the King's decree, their meetings were often short and he would ride from the wood upon his horse, promising to return as soon as he was able. She never knew where he went during these absences, only that she counted the moments until his return.

Even during his trips, the trees stayed quiet and Willow had never been more lonely. Finally, during one of these separations, she could stand the silence of her adopted family no longer. She called to them, "Friends! Why have you forsaken me, the one you embraced, raised and loved? How have I wronged you?"

As a breeze danced and lifted her hair from her shoulders, her family returned to her once more. But she shivered, sensing a coolness in their energy and they bent forward in despair, their branches brushing her cheek, for they had sad news.

"Child, the man you love is a bringer of war. He leads your father's armies on violent quests, destroying villages and ravaging all the lands he touches. Your father cares not for the beauty of this country, only of possessing it. Under his orders, this man will lead the army on a quest that will bring a war like this land has never seen. It will move swiftly from one kingdom to the next, unstoppable, destroying all it touches. Enemies of your father are tired of his relentless wars and will join together to stop him, eventually journeying here, sentencing this land, and us, to destruction."

Shaking her head violently at this proclamation, she begged them to take it back, to tell her they were lying while at the same time knowing that the trees were incapable of lies.

Soon, he returned to her, and Willow fell into his arms, refusing to meet his gaze. "My dear, is it true you are a general in my father's army?"

He had heard the stories of her protests against her father's war campaigns and he knew he could not bring himself to answer and lose her forever. His silence answered her question and she fell to her knees in the moss, her heart broken. Crushed by this new pain, she retreated into the hollow of the closest tree and remained there for a fortnight.

The trees did their best to bring comfort to their heartbroken child's ailing heart. Their branches twisted and danced harder, determined to pull her from her despair. The surrounding villages declared they had never seen such winds and spoke of an oncoming storm. Those at the castle spoke of oncoming war.

With Willow still lost in her sadness, the trees still dancing with their pleas, the army gathered. The king declared that war must be waged on a nearby kingdom and his most ruthless general was ordered to lead the troops into battle.

Sensing the coming army, the trees intensified their call to their daughter. Their arms waved violently and their whispers turned to deep howls.

"Child, the army is coming and soon we will be destroyed." From inside her dark shelter, Willow lifted her head. "Please, do not let your kind destroy us." The trees, who only ever gave, never asking for anything in return, now turned to her for help. It was this act of desperation that pulled Willow into action.

The ground shook under the hooves of the approaching horses, and the winds nudged her as she emerged from the tree line. She left behind the safety of the trees and stepped into the storm, directly in front of the impending army.

Poised at the head of a mass of horses and armor was a regal and gallant man, the only human she had ever loved. Willow stood before him and his army and told him he could not pass. At first, she pleaded, begging him to turn back, to understand that his mission would end in destruction for all. He shook his head, his arguments almost lost to the winds. His orders came from her father, and her father was king.

"My father knows only war," she shouted above the howls. "You cannot trust a man who knows nothing of peace and contentment."

He paused to consider her words and she saw the love they once shared flickering behind his eyes, but there was also conflict. Duty and honor stifled the light she had come to love.

She closed her eyes and bowed her head, knowing that her pleas and arguments would hold no merit with this eternal soldier. She opened her eyes again, looking into his face, and the storm howled in response. Her hair, that often danced softly in the wind, lifted from her shoulders. Her eyes remained fixed on his as her dark hair twisted and danced, reaching down her back, past her knees, twirling through the air. It met the hanging arms of the trees surrounding her and the watching army could no longer tell where her hair ended and the branches began.

As they watched in awed fascination, Willow's skin took on the dark hue of the mossy limbs and she was lifted from the ground, branches wrapping around her, she wrapping around the branches. They began to retreat in horror but their general pushed forward. Above the wind, they could hear him calling to the girl.

Branches thrashed violently and a high-pitched wail joined the deep howl of the storm's winds. The army would swear it was the girl screaming, but they could no longer see her. For she was gone and where once she stood, they saw only green, whipping wildly, closer and closer to the general crying into the wind from his horse.

His men yelled at him to turn back but it was too late. He too was lifted and the branches engulfed him in an almost passionate embrace.

After the great storm, peace fell over the land. Whispered rumors filled the villages, claiming the woods had cursed any army that dared to break the peace of their shelter. A terrified army abandoned the king and without men to lead, the lost warrior slipped slowly into madness and his castle fell silent.

And in the woods, those looking closely enough could find two new trees, their branches dancing happily on the breeze.

The Halfway House

He emerges from a cloud of steam; the simmering dish grasped firmly between two oven mitts. "It's ready," he exclaims triumphantly, and the table buzzes with excitement. The faces lining the long table watch my father's dance from the stove to the table and back and soon a patchwork of steaming delicacies fills the wooden surface in front of us.

Our guests have only recently arrived, and I don't know them yet. I don't know which foods will capture their hearts, so I watch. The elderly woman across from me smiles at a plate of chocolate chip cookies and her eyes close as she remembers.

I look toward the end of the table, where a middle-aged gentleman is shaking his head at a roast. "Every Sunday," he mutters, "every single Sunday." I wonder who will go first. It's a little game I play with myself at our evening meals and tonight my bet is on the old woman eyeing the cookies.

Up and down the table, through the steam of the bubbling mac and cheese and the smoke coming from the slightly burned garlic bread, I hear murmurs, exclamations of nostalgia as the food works its magic. They're all making progress, but it's the elderly woman who, when she opens her eyes again, is gazing past me into the life that was now surely playing out before her.

"My granddaughter loves baking cookies" she whispers, uncertain that anyone is listening. When she sees me watching her, she smiles kindly and continues. "She's about your age, barely a teenager but still willing to spend time with an old woman. Such a good little cook…"

As she tells me about her granddaughter's first time baking, the flour everywhere after the bag broke, the care she took to measure each ingredient perfectly, she begins to fade. I can see the back of the chair through her chest, and I nod along, encouraging her to continue her story even as her voice echoes as though from the end of a tunnel. With each word, she disappears into the backdrop of the kitchen, until she is gone.

When my father finally takes his seat, he is the only one to reach forward and spoon food onto his plate. By that time, two of our five guests have disappeared and the man at the end of the table, muttering about the roast, is already a wispy, fading outline.

My father looks pleased with his work as he shoves a forkful of mac and cheese into his mouth and nods. The dishes were full, but he didn't cook to feed their hunger—everyone knows ghosts don't eat. He cooked to feed their memories.

He glances at me and winks, and I hear his explanation of many years ago echo in my head. Right after they started showing up, he'd

24

told me, "They're a little lost when they die, Pearl. They don't remember who they were in life, so they don't know where they belong in death. Food helps. Food always helps."

For as long as I can remember, our home at the edge of the Lakewood Cemetery has been a stopping point for souls passing on to the next realm. As the caretaker of the cemetery, my father wasn't even disturbed when the ghosts started wandering up the front steps into the house. "Well, I take care of the cemetery, I guess it's my job to take care of its residents, too."

"That was a highly successful meal don't you think, Pearl?" he asks, pushing back his plate and standing. There are only two guests left, and they look from the food to my father to me, just as lost as when they'd first arrived. For some special cases, food isn't enough. Even if they remember who they were, something else keeps them from passing.

I nod and stand too.

"You folks can head on upstairs and find a room that suits you. Pearl will be up shortly to make sure you've settled in."

While my father clears the mostly untouched dishes off the table, the two figures rise, and I motion them toward the main staircase. They glide past me, their feet moving as though they're walking even though they hover just a few inches above the ground. It takes some time to get used to being dead.

"I'll be up soon," I say. It was my job to help the guests when the food failed. For some reason, they always seemed to trust me. When I talked to them, asked them questions, they opened up, and they remembered.

Before I can head up after them, there's a sound just outside the front door that shakes the foundation of the house. I jump and look to my father, who has hurried from the kitchen and now stands in the entryway. *Bam. Bam.* I open the door.

The massive, bearded man is dragging an ax behind him as he climbs the porch steps, the blade banging against each stair. *Bam. Bam.* The sound sets my teeth on edge. It's an effort for him to take the last step and I imagine he must be newly dead because he's still moving like his body aches. He scales the last step, and as he approaches the door, my father moves in front of me.

None of the ghosts have ever tried to hurt me, but there's something different about this one. His heavy-lidded eyes look out through a mess of curls and facial hair. His thick, plaid shirt is torn, and one side of his suspenders droops off his shoulder.

The lumberjack enters the house and pauses for a moment, looking around. He glances at my father, then at me. His gaze freezes on me for a moment, and my father moves again to block me from his view. After a few blinks, the man walks forward, dragging his ax behind him, and starts up the stairs. *Thump. Thump.* A shudder goes through me, and my teeth chatter.

My father looks down at me. "Leave this one alone, please." He's never asked me to do that.

But I can't leave the man alone. It's my job to help them. So, when my father goes back to the kitchen to clean up and prepare for our next round of guests, I move up the stairs.

The lumberjack is in one of the guest rooms, pacing, the ax screeching as it drags against the wood floor. I step into the room but he keeps his eyes low.

"Hello."

He grunts. When he finally looks at me, it's only for a moment before he glances furtively away.

"What brought you to us?" I ask.

The man shrugs. He looks up at me again, and this time his gaze lingers.

"What's the last thing you remember?"

He shrugs again. He's looking at me like I'm a puzzle he's trying to solve. I shift, uncomfortable under his scrutinizing stare. He notices and turns away, wandering over to the window. He looks beyond the cemetery, to the trees surrounding us.

"From the woods..." His voice is gravelly and hard to understand.

"What's that?"

"I came from the woods."

"Oh. Good."

He jerks his head back to study me again, and his rough voice declares, "You look…"

"Pearl!" My father appears in the doorway. "I told you to leave our visitor alone."

I sigh and move toward the door, turning my back on the lumberjack. But before I reach the exit, I hear a clatter of wood against wood. Without looking, I know he's dropped the ax and I hear him whisper, "You…"

I turn to face him. His eyes are wide, and his form is flickering as though he's shaking.

He whispers, "It was an accident."

"What was?" I ask, but I know.

"I should head back to the house," she thinks. But she loves the woods at dusk. The cool of the evening is prickling her cheeks, and the birds dancing in the trees sing their final songs of the day. Just a few more minutes, she tells herself, she'll head back before dark.

Dusk falls faster than she expects and soon it's hard to see the ground in front of her. She stumbles over a stick as she turns back toward the house. Dinner is probably ready. Since her mother died, her father puts so much work into their dinners, tries so hard to take care of her.

She can't see the house, but she knows these woods, the woods sheltering their cemetery. Before she can begin her progress through the coming dark, she hears something. Whop, whop. *The sound vibrates the trees and makes her teeth chatter. It's coming from nearby, but she can't see through the thickening darkness.*

The sound gets louder as she treads carefully through the dark woods. And then, it stops. She hears a rustling, a shifting of leaves and stops walking. There's an explosion of white light as the back of her head expands with pain and she feels the sharp edges of dried leaves meet her cheeks.

She lays among the twigs and leaves, something warm and sticky slowly flowing around her head, and thinks of her father. He took care of her. If she left him now, who would he take care of? She could feel herself slipping away and she fought it. She knew her body wouldn't make it, she could already feel the life draining from her limbs, but somehow she knew she didn't have to go to the place she was being called. She could stay. And she would.

"You shouldn't have been working in the dark." My father's voice is harsh. "You were careless, and you took her from me." His tone softens. "I heard on the news they found you at the bottom of a tree.

They said you left a note, that you'd lived with the guilt for too long and couldn't do it anymore."

I look between the two of them, overtly aware of my body for the first time in a long time. I feel light. I look down. My feet hover inches off the ground.

My father turns to me. "You showed up right after the funeral. Just walked in like it was any other day and sat at the table. So, I made you dinner. You didn't eat, but it seemed to comfort you, and you enjoyed talking to me while I cooked and ate. Then, the others came. They were different. This wasn't their home; it was simply a stopping point. They needed help and comfort like you did, so I cooked for them, too. They trusted you because they saw who you were, even if you couldn't. Together, we helped them move on."

Grief flashes in his eyes, but it's an old grief, and I wonder how long I've been holding on. He turns back to the lumberjack, who's staring at me, pain raging behind his eyes. My father swallows and squares his shoulders. "I know it was an accident. You never meant to hurt her." He sighs, letting go of his anger, "I forgive you."

And just like that, the storm behind the lumberjack's eyes calms, and the dark red and black of his shirt blends with the wood grain in the wall behind him. With one last glance at me, he offers a half-smile and crosses into his next life.

My father turns to me. "Thank you for letting me take care of you, Pearl. Thank you for helping me take care of the others, but you don't have to do it anymore. I can do it alone. I'll be okay."

Then, it's like I drop a weight I didn't know I've been carrying. My guilt hits the floor like the lumberjack's ax and I am weightless. I reach out to touch my father, but I can't see my hand. I watch his smile until it fades away and then, I too am okay.

The Date

"The walls in here are so bright."

"No, I'm sorry I don't have a light! I didn't know you smoked."

"Smoke? No, they're too pink for that. More like a coral."

I moaned under my breath from my spot at the bar. It's easier for me to hear the uncomfortable exchange than it is for the people actually having it.

"Move on," I mumbled around the edge my martini glass. I watched in the mirror behind the bar as the man caught on to their predicament and shifted his seat closer to his date.

"Is that better?" he asked.

"Better than what?"

"Never mind," he laughed. "Do you like your wine?"

I cringed inwardly and willed the conversation to go another direction. *Don't talk about going to the bathroom, don't talk about going to the ...*

"Oh, it's lovely. I just have to drink it slow or I'll be going to the bathroom all night."

I sighed but he laughed a big booming laugh.

"I know what you mean. One can of beer means all night in the can for me!"

Okay, that was clever, I thought but I heard a groan from beside me. I looked over but the man next to me was staring down into his beer.

I tuned back into their conversation in time to hear her say, "Well, that's all well and good, but with my hip it takes me just as long to get to the bathroom as it does to actually go."

"Oh, come on…" this time I said it out loud but luckily not loud enough for the geriatric daters.

"Next he's gonna start talking about his medications."

I jumped at the voice but at the table behind me, the old man responded to something I hadn't heard. "I believe it. I don't know which pill does what, I just know I haven't peed right since the nineties."

Another groan. I looked over as the mystery man took a long pull of his beer.

"I'm sorry, do I know you?" I asked, confused that another human would have has much interest in this train wreck of a date as I did.

"Doubt it," he said, "But I'm guessing you know the saucy minx at the table behind us."

"I…"

"I'm Nathan. That's my Grandpa Gabe."

"Oh," I said, "I'm Amy. That's my Grandma Rose."

34

He nodded as though it were completely normal to follow your grandparent on a date and eavesdrop on their conversation.

"So, what do you think? Take a drink every time they mention medication, aching joints, or technology they can't work?"

I laughed. "That seems dangerous."

"But fun," he said, motioning to the bartender, "Another round of drinks, please…" From behind us, Grandma Rose's voice carried across the restaurant, "I swear I haven't been able to turn my TV off for a week!"

"Better keep 'em coming!" Nathan winked.

A few rounds later, after they'd touched on Facebook, trying to ask Alexa questions, and discussing the weather's impact on each limb, the couple decided they needed a bathroom break. Nathan and I were leaned in with our heads together, waiting for the next topic, when Gabe stood up.

"Oh, thank goodness," I sighed. "I need a break."

Nathan laughed and ordered us a couple of waters.

"So," he said, sliding mine toward me, "what prompts a woman your age to stalk her grandmother's date instead of pursuing her own?"

"I could ask you the same question."

He shrugged, "You could, and the answer is simple, I love my grandpa and he's been pretty lonely since Gram died. I knew if I didn't do something he'd sit in his big house, in front of his old TV watching *M.A.S.H* reruns, and yelling at Alexa until it was time to join Gram."

I nodded, "Similar story."

"So, I pulled up that Silver Years dating thing, he saw a picture of your grandma, grumbled that she had a nice smile, and I set the connection in motion. But now, he paused, raising an eyebrow at me. "I'm guessing that when I sent that winky face it was not Rose that sent back the blushing face."

I held up my hands innocently. "Hey, she did actually blush when I said someone winked at her."

He laughed, a booming laugh like his grandpa's. It made me smile.

"I've been living with Grandma since my divorce and it's been a saving grace for both of us but, someday, I'm going to want to move out and move on. I couldn't stand the thought of her watching *ER* and *Call the Midwife* by herself. But I also couldn't stand the thought of her getting out there for the first time all alone. It's silly, I guess…"

He lifted his water glass toward me, "Not silly at all."

I lifted mine too and we clinked.

From the corner of my eye, I saw Grandma Rose shuffling back to the table with Gabe not far behind her. I nudged Nathan and we shifted toward each other, leaning backward to listen. Immediately, I could sense a shift in the mood at the table. I snuck a glance behind me and I saw Grandma sigh as she settled into her seat, looking around the room as though she were looking back through time.

"Oh, this place…" she said.

"Oh god," I whispered, recognizing the change in her tone.

The panic in Nathan's eyes mirrored mine. "Dead spouses?" he asked.

"Dead spouses."

He shook his head and took a drink of his beer.

I tried not to listen but after a minute, I heard my name. "It's been so nice having her there but I know she can't stay forever. It's just been lovely not to be so lonely."

I snuck a glance behind me and saw Gabe nod knowingly and then lean over the table.

"You don't have to be lonely." He placed a hand over hers.

I turned away and sighed, trying to hide the tears lining my eyes.

"Is this what we have to look forward to if we're still dating in our eighties?" I asked softly.

"Well," said Nathan, "I guess we better make sure that doesn't happen."

He placed his hand over mine.

Freedom

The knife. Grab the knife. But he couldn't hear me because my lips weren't moving. My stomach burned like it always did when I tried to take control, the flame of her presence igniting and spreading further the more I tried to fight. That was the strangest part about the whole thing: being possessed by a demon felt like nothing more than a bad case of indigestion.

"Why are you here?" she snarled through my lips.

He stepped closer to my body and I could smell crisp air and dying leaves on his coat. Was it fall already? Time was doing strange things. I tried to scream as he studied my face, looking for any sign that I was still there. She gave none. His shoulders sagged. "I came to tell you that this is my last visit."

As she threw my head back and laughed, I deflated. I should have expected this. He shouldn't have to live with this creature as his wife. It was over for us the moment she took control.

She refused to touch him. She barely talked to him. He'd thought I was leaving him. Until the day her true reflection showed in the mirror. He'd tried to save me, but what could he do? Once he knew the truth, she wouldn't let him stay in the house. But he kept coming back, kept trying.

This was the closest he'd been to us in months. I could smell him. I couldn't do this. I wanted out no matter what it took. *The knife*, I tried again, trying to convince my head to turn toward the bedside table where the blade glinted in the fall light coming through the curtains.

"You're *leaving* her?" she taunted. She was enjoying her victory and I took advantage of her distraction. Instead of focusing on taking over completely, I turned all my energy to my hand, the hand closest to the knife. The knife she always kept by her side. The knife she coveted but was afraid of. I couldn't read her thoughts, but I felt her fear whenever that knife was out of sight.

"I'm not leaving her. She's already gone."

I wasn't gone, but I could be. I could be free. *Twitch*, I urged my fingers. *Move. Point.*

And then one did. It twitched, ever so slightly, toward the knife and, drawn to the movement, his eyes fell to the weapon. She felt it too and her anger burned. They both lunged but maybe my control was stronger for a moment because he got there first.

He didn't hesitate. He didn't say goodbye. There wasn't time. He simply lifted the knife, brought it down, and set me free.

The Last Cry

Claire didn't get up when she heard the baby cry. Her lids lifted, revealing the dark room that had once more slipped into silence, the echo of the infant's cry reverberating off the walls. Her head fell to the side, and her eyes settled on the empty space next to her. Eric was up. She heard the floorboards creak under his determined steps. She waited for the cry to come again.

There it was. Sharp, but strained. A long wail and then a gurgle. Offended and then desperate, demanding a response. But it wasn't time yet so she didn't move. She heard Eric descend the stairs and knew she had a brief respite before she would hear it again.

With a deep breath, she pulled her legs out from under the covers. They fell over the edge of the bed, and she used the momentum to pull herself into a sitting position. Her heart, which had been furiously beating since the first cry, finally began to slow. The fierce beat drumming against her rib cage was the only reminder of the reaction that cry used to evoke.

She heard the soft music from the floor below that meant Eric's nightly routine had officially begun. She could picture him as he went from the stereo to the couch, heard him sit heavily, heard the clink of the liquor decanter bumping against his glass. After this drink, he would come back upstairs.

He didn't know she was awake, she was sure. She never told him what his nightly haunts did to her. She never told him that she heard the cry every time and that it woke her every night. She never let him know that in the first few days it had even brought on her milk, causing her to hate her own body for its betrayal. He never knew that for months after it caused her to throw her legs over the side of the bed, driven by an unfed instinct before her conscious mind could take over and tell her there was no reason to move. He didn't know she'd had to train herself to ignore it. Eventually she had, and she'd stopped pulling herself out of bed, stopped being dragged toward the sound. Now, the wail only reminded her of that day.

She'd been pushing for hours. The excitement that surfaced with the quick gush of water and the frequent pains had deteriorated little by little with each long hour. Each strained push convinced her something was wrong and the joy of the day was replaced with fear and uncertainty.

Claire jumped at the creak of the stairs and watched the closed bedroom door. On the other side, she knew he was moving back upstairs, back to the nursery, unaware that she was tracking his movements from her spot on the bed, waiting patiently for her turn to enter the room. There was no need to rush; she could let him have this last night.

She heard the door and listened to him move into the room and pause. There it was again. Her heart pounded but she blocked the rush of memories threatening to derail her. Her hand flew to her chest and then slid down to her stomach and paused, anchoring her to the moment, her mission. Tonight was too important to let memories confuse and distract her. She needed to stay focused.

The cry faded and she heard a deep sigh as Eric sank into the rocking chair that had never been removed from the nursery. She could see his routine play out in front of her as though it were a movie she'd watched too many times. Every night, he crawled into bed next to her, as though they were any other couple, ending their day side by side. She would fall asleep listening to his uneven breathing, knowing he was still awake. She usually slept until the first cry but she didn't know if he ever did. Then, with the sound, her eyes opened and she became a silent observer of his nightly haunts, an outsider simply watching his life.

In the mornings, she would watch him leave for work, where, she assumed, he tended to the kids he served as principal, just like he always had. She watched him come home in the evenings and observed him from across the dinner table. They might talk, but he wasn't there. He was upstairs. His eyes would dart upward every few minutes, his fingers twitching as though reaching for the playback button. He was an addict waiting for his next fix, counting down the moments until he could satisfy it. She didn't know why, but he never went in during the day. It was only at night, when the world was quiet, that he fed his addiction.

And then there were the nights of desperation. The nights he crawled back into bed just as the first flickers of dawn were dancing across the room, shaking, clammy and utterly exhausted. He would slide under the covers, move until his chest was pressed against her back and his arms would snake around her in a vice-like grip. It was in these moments she knew reality had truly caught up with him, and she grasped his hands and held him to her. *"It's all right,"* she tried to tell him on those nights, passing the message through her body and into his. *"We will be okay."* They never spoke.

Sometimes, they were husband and wife again; clinging to each other, making love in order to shut out the cruel joke life had played on them, trying in vain to recapture what they once were. For a few moments, they were united in their grief instead of separate. They were together, and Claire would find hope in this union. Until the next night when, without fail, the nightmare would begin again. The nightmare that had started the moment Eric had accepted the doctor's offer.

They knew the possibilities, of course. How could they not, when modern medicine stared at them from glass cases everywhere they went? Claire faced these advances every time she visited the neighbors' house and was greeted with the icy, blank eyes of their teenage son and heard him yell, "Catch, Luke!" The last thing he had shouted before the car hit him five years ago.

She shuddered at these medical advancements every time she stepped into her mother's house and heard her grandmother's shaky whisper, "I love you." Her mother thought Claire would find comfort in hearing the woman's last words every time she entered or exited the house. But Claire was too disgusted by the suspended body, floating, frozen as though she had been about to take a step, to find any solace in those glassy eyes.

It seemed no one, when given an alternative, was ready to let go. Only a few years ago, they'd had no other choice. The chambers were practically household staples at this point, a piece of furniture or decor that adorned almost every home, because almost everyone had lost someone. They said it was a way to preserve the body until a cure could be found for whatever was killing them, or until medicine caught up with their injuries. Claire had always seen it as a strange and eerie way to display the dead, to hold on to their memory, and she'd thought that Eric agreed. But grief made you do strange things.

She had been pushing for so long, gripping Eric's hand in one of hers and the bed frame with the other, beads of sweat pouring off her face and soaking her hospital gown. Eric was saying something about being strong. That she was strong and the baby was strong and they could both do this and everything would be okay. But she knew it wouldn't.

"Something has gone wrong. The effort of the birth has put too much strain on the heart." That's what they said before the final push. The push that would bring forth a dying child; the life they'd been awaiting for nine months would be gone after only a few moments of life.

And then...there she was. It was almost as if nothing were wrong. She was wriggling and slimy and had all her fingers and toes, even if she was a little too blue. Claire pulled the child to her chest and she squalled just like a normal baby, screaming at the top of her lungs at the indecency of it all. Claire knew exactly how she felt. And then, the cry changed. It became strained, as though someone was squeezing off her airway, and she began to gurgle as though she had swallowed water. And then she was being pulled away from Claire, and the doctors offered a solution.

She never understood the appeal. When the procedure became common practice, Claire made it quite clear she would never be interested. When it became regulation for every adult to sign a waiver either requesting or denying the procedure, she was adamant. No matter what fate may befall her, she would pass. She couldn't help the poor souls that were already encapsulated, and she couldn't change the minds of the families that chose to entrap them, but she refused to be one of them. Eric had nodded, equally disturbed by the thought. He would honor her wishes, he'd said, stroking her hair and assuring her that he didn't understand either, just didn't see the point. Until he did.

"Yes," he said, his hand falling out of Claire's as he stepped toward this last ray of hope, "We'll do it."

The doctor tried to hide his shock but Claire saw the corner of his mouth turn down and his eyebrows furrow for a moment before he rearranged his face back to its impartial mask. He turned to Claire, silently pleading with her to do something. Preservation on an infant was almost unheard of. But Claire didn't have the strength to argue. She was exhausted, distraught. There were still tears mixed with beads of sweat drying on her cheeks and her dark hair was matted to her forehead. She didn't argue, she simply shrugged and nodded.

Yes, they would allow their moments-old child to be preserved in a cryogenic chamber to await the day, which might never come, when there would be a breakthrough in modern medicine that could revive her.

"We want the projection feature, too." Eric's voice was unnecessarily loud and the doctor winced. The doctor was picturing the Hell their life would become when the only sound they could ever hear from their child was its last, strangled cry.

A few months after that day, Claire tried to talk to Eric. She'd told him she needed to mourn the child, to move on. He'd insisted there was no reason to mourn. Soon, there would be a cure, a way to bring her back and they wouldn't have to say goodbye. They wouldn't have to move on.

"But for how long?" she'd asked, trying to remind him of the conversations they'd had so many times before about the futile hopes wrapped up in the preservations. "What if it takes thirty years?"

"Is there a limit to how long you will wait for your own child?"

Claire had retreated into silence after that. But yes, she thought, standing up, there was a limit. This hellish ordeal had to end and that morning she'd realized it would have to end soon. When she saw that blue plus sign on the stick in front of her, she once again felt excitement stir. Excitement that had been buried since that day three years ago. Excitement…and hope. She dared to let herself hope once again. And that hope begged for action.

It wasn't fair to her; it wasn't fair to him. They were both so tired. She and Eric deserved a second chance, the child in the room next to her deserved peace and the child inside her deserved a chance at a normal life. But there was no way any of them would get what they needed while this continued.

She went to the bedroom door and, before opening it, pressed her ear against it. He'd been in the nursery for at least twenty minutes; his drink would soon be empty. Right on cue, she heard the chair creak as he stood and went toward the chamber. It was coming, but this time she didn't brace herself against it. She closed her eyes and let the harsh wail that had once reverberated against her chest wash over her. The hopeless siren of an ending life. She took it in, recorded it in her own mind and knew she would never forget it. It was the last time she would hear her child cry.

When it was over, she heard the door groan and his footsteps tread to the stairs. After a series of protests from the old wood, he was downstairs and the rattle of the ice machine told her he was there to stay. Without pausing to give it another thought, she pushed open the bedroom door.

Outside the nursery, she paused. She hadn't entered the room in at least two years. In the beginning, she'd gone in occasionally, but she found it brought her no comfort. It wasn't a grave, it wasn't a memorial. It was purgatory in their own home.

With a deep breath, she pushed open the nursery door. It was just as it had been in the months before the birth. The crib they had assembled together stood against the wall in front of her, the rocking chair in the corner to the right. The dresser with the hand-painted flowers stood to her left, filled with pink onesies, tiny polka dot pants and topped with a dusty ballerina lamp.

Slipping into the room, she pulled the door quietly shut behind her. Without the glow from the hall, the only light came from the dim gleam of the chamber. She approached the capsule and knew there would be no pause, no trepidation. She had said her goodbyes years ago, had begun her mourning period when she'd felt the life leave the small body pressed against her chest. This figure, this floating statue in front of her was not her daughter—this was a science experiment.

With one last glance at the icy form, and a silent prayer that peace would find the pacing figure downstairs, she reached down toward the wall and gripped the rubber plug.

"Goodnight, sleep now." And she unplugged the chamber.

The Dragon Killer

The penalty for killing a dragon was death, but when I killed one, I was granted eternal life.

I too was close to death when I came across the injured beast. Our dimming life lights must have called to each other across the dark forest as I searched for a way to live, he for a way to die.

The illness raging inside me pulled me from my village, where healers of spirit and science alike had placed their hands upon my cheek and dropped their gaze to deliver the news that I was beyond help. As is custom in my village, I bid my family farewell, left all my earthly belongings behind, and set out on my death journey to find and greet the great creator.

The tears of my children soaked into my clothes as I hugged and kissed them and their mother. The salt had not yet dried on the rough fabric when I decided I was not ready to die. This journey would not be one of death, but of life. I still had a little strength left in my ravaged body and I would use it to seek a cure. Surely there was someone, some saint or spirit or shaman, that could pull this vile disease from my blood and give me back my life. I did not speak of my plan to my family but I made a silent promise that I would once again return to them, and then I set off on my journey.

I traveled as fast as my failing body would allow and stopped in each village I came across. I sought out not only healers, but scientists and men of the creator and those who looked to the stars for guidance. All said the same thing: My life, the life I knew, was coming to an end.

I was between villages when I felt the earth rumbling beneath my feet. It had been weeks since I'd left home and my body was failing me. I hadn't even the strength to build a fire and the falling night was quickly sapping the warmth from the earth. My body shook from the cold. I could feel death approaching and knew my journey was coming to an end. I would not be able to keep my silent promise to my family.

The rumbling traveled through my legs and my knees gave out from under me. My face met the floor of the darkening forest and that was when I felt the heat. The ground beneath me warmed my body like a blanket and my chills subsided long enough for me to lift my head toward a deep rumbling, the source of the quivering earth. As I pulled my body closer to the sound, the strength of the heat grew. It felt like fire but I saw no orange glow, heard no crackling of kindling. Finally, I dragged myself through a grove of trees and came to a clearing where I found myself face to face with the beast that would forever alter my life.

52

I couldn't have run if I wanted to but I immediately knew this dragon was no threat to me. His head was taller than I was, and his body stretched behind him so far I couldn't find his tail in the coming night. He could have killed me with one swipe of his massive claws, or with one chomp of his great jaw, but I knew, when his glassy eyes met mine, that I had nothing to fear.

Perhaps it was because I was in the same state, but somehow I could sense his pain. I took stock of his massive form, inspecting it for the cause of his discomfort—I found it. Jammed into his side, a piece of wood longer and thicker than me. Whatever blade or point was on the end was shoved so far into his great gut that I could not see it, but I knew it must have been sharp to puncture the thick skin of a dragon. His breath came in shallow gasps and each exhale let forth a blast of warm air that shook the ground and warmed it at the same time. I pulled myself into a sitting position in front of his snout and, without thinking, placed a hand on his cheek just as the healers and spirit guides and men of the stars had done to me.

"Your life is failing, beast," I whispered into the dark.

His deep sigh was the only confirmation I needed.

"As is mine." I leaned against the side of his face, letting him support me. "It is time to let go."

But he did not relax into death as I was now prepared to do. He shook his snout, pushing me forward, and a deep groan, of what I imagined was frustration, escaped his throat. It was then that a long-buried piece of knowledge resurfaced.

"A dragon's life force is eternal. They roamed the Earth long before us and will remain long after we are gone. Their breath heats the earth and their wings bring the wind. Their hearts are pure and any act of violence against such a creature is an act punishable by death."

I sat up. "You cannot die." I did not ask but simply stated this sad, undeniable fact. The great creatures would not die naturally, but they could be injured, even killed. The dragon blinked slowly in response. His body was weak. His injury was debilitating, so that he could not fly nor eat nor lift himself from this spot we shared ... nor could he die.

I bowed my head in shame. "I am sorry, my friend. Here I have been fighting, wanting nothing more than to live while you want nothing more than to die."

While it was an unforgivable crime to harm a dragon, many farmers did not want them near their fields, and so they set traps that would go off if the winged-beasts flew too close, but still let the great creatures walk away. They thought it kept them innocent, since they'd never put hand to leathery hide. I now saw, first-hand, that their tricks were anything but.

Pulling me from my thoughts, there was a great rustling of sticks and leaves and earth to my right. I turned to find his claw raking at the ground; it was the only part of his body, besides his eyes, that moved. I

54

looked to his face and back to his claw in confusion. He was trying to tell me something I could not understand. Then, it seemed he used the last of his remaining strength to bend his claw so far forward that the nail digging into the ground snapped and fell away from his body. He moaned in pain and the air flowing from his snout grew hotter, but he was beyond fire-breathing.

From beside me, he shifted his snout, pushing my body toward the discarded claw, the only weapon available to us. I looked into his eye and knew what he was asking me to do.

"I cannot," I shook my head. "Do not ask it. Such an act is unforgivable and the punishment is death." But even as I spoke the words, I knew how feeble they sounded coming from a dying man. Why should I fear death?

I stepped toward him and placed my hand once again on the side of his face, ready to ask if there was any other way, anything else I could do to help, and there, in the corner of his eye sat a tear the size of my head. As I watched, it dropped from his eye and slid down the scaly surface of his nose. It fell onto my hand, soaking the sleeve of my jacket just as the tears of my children had on the day I'd left home. If I could not have my own wish to return to them, I could at least grant a final wish to this dying creature.

With my head bowed in reverence, asking forgiveness for what I was about to do, I used what strength I had to lift the dragon's claw and grip it in my hands. Before I could wonder as to the best place to deliver the fateful blow, the dragon craned his neck, exposing the vulnerable skin underneath. After one last grateful look, the dragon closed his eyes, relaxing into death when I lifted the claw with a newfound strength and brought it down into the soft, tight skin of his beautiful neck.

There was no blood that day in the woods—the day I broke the law we'd all been taught since we were children. When the neck of the dragon was punctured and I invited death to take this once deathless creature, there was a great flash of light. Of course, I thought it was the light guiding me to the other side, that the effort had drained me and that I would join the creature whose life I was taking. But it was not.

I did not die that day, nor the next, or the next. In fact, I got stronger. With that flash of light, the body of the dragon disappeared, melting into the Earth and returning to the creator. And I seemed to find the cure I was looking for; my body regained its strength. All of my pain melted away and on two sturdy legs, I walked out of the forest I had practically crawled into.

I returned to my family a miracle, the man who had beaten death. I reentered my peaceful life, working the fields, raising my children, and making love to my wife. When her hair began to turn gray and mine did not, I did not wonder at it. When her back began to stoop and I stayed upright, however, and her skin began to wrinkle and mine stayed smooth, the village began to talk. As my children grew and had children of their own and my wife's health failed, I sensed that my own friends feared me. The children I had fought to live for now shirked away from my touch and I knew this was no longer my home. Once again, I said goodbye to my family, kissed my dying wife, and left the only home I had ever known.

And then, the next dragon came. I was once again drawn to another dying creature as I made my way through the woods and I knew what life now held for me.

I am the dragon killer. They come to me in pain and I, the man with no fear of death, put an end to their suffering. When I killed that first dragon I was seeking a way to live and he, grateful for the mercy I showed him, granted me my wish. I will never die. I will spend my life helping others die while I go on living. It is my life's work. It is my gift ... and my curse.

A Birthday

9:05 a.m.

They all stare at me as they sing. Some of them mean it, I can tell. They've been here long enough and they know how I'm feeling right now. Some stare at me but don't see me, their eyes as glassy and unfocused as mine must be. Most of them are off-key. But hey, beggars can't be choosers, and drunks are lucky to get any sort of birthday celebration at all.

I stare awkwardly down at the table and try to remember the last birthday I was actually sober. It certainly wasn't this one.

I had planned to stop drinking by forty and if I had, I wouldn't be spending the big four-oh in the hospital's involuntary admittance program, listening to a bunch of strangers sing happy birthday instead of my family.

They all stop singing at different times and on different notes and I try to smile my thanks. My lips are dry and cracked. There's no cake. Nobody hands me a cigar. I could use a drink.

The first day in rehab, not much happens. My first day in this program was my fifth or sixth first day—I've lost count at this point.

You get the good drugs and you're groggy and lethargic throughout orientation. It's almost like being drunk. Almost.

Then you get sick.

I woke up on my second day with diarrhea and nausea, worse than any hangover I've ever had. It's almost worth staying drunk forever just to avoid this moment, this feeling...but I guess that kind of thinking is what got me here in the first place.

I was depressed, too. *That* lasts a while.

Today, my birthday, has been a little better, but it might not be completely better for a long time. Maybe ever. I've done some damage. To myself. To my wife ... my kids. Those poor kids. Thank god they're still so small but Mary ... oh, Mary.

I've been drinking since I was a teenager, since I first started performing on stage and my hands shook too much to hold a guitar. Now I'm forty. There's no changing what I've already done, but maybe I can stop it from happening again. I *have* to stop it from happening again or I risk losing everything—my family, my friends, my life...

Because drinking *will* kill you. Rehab has taught me that. Watching myself waste away has taught me that.

You do it hard enough, for long enough, it will turn your body into something you never imagined it could be. A gaunt, pale, wispy, trembling version of yourself. A ghost of the person you once were, complete with translucent skin, a haunting cry, a poor memory, and most likely *a lot* of unfinished business.

11:00 a.m.

Right after breakfast, a big black man named Ishmael taught us about fear. Apparently, I'm afraid to change and I'm afraid of who I am without drugs and alcohol. Sounds about right. I don't actually remember the last time I wasn't afraid and I've *never* liked being myself...my father didn't much like me being myself either. But that's a story for another therapy session.

Every bad situation in my life that caused me to drink only happened because I was too afraid to change it. How's that for self-awareness?

Another speaker talked about addicts as misdirected artists. Now that's definitely me. I spent years drinking before shows, to kill the anxiety, preparing to put on an act, change my personality, make people like me...somewhere along the way, I got lost in that act.

6:00 p.m.

I got to see my family after dinner. My little girl's voice is the sweetest music I know, and I've played *a lot* of music.

When I saw her, I picked her up and tossed her into the air. She's older than her little brother but still lighter and she squealed as she left my hands for the briefest of moments. When she came back to me again, my arms shook and my legs almost gave out beneath me. In my head, her happy squeal had turned into the panicked scream I heard the last time I was in the car with her.

Nobody noticed my legs falter and I slid easily into the chair behind me. I pulled her to my chest, remembering the sound of tires squealing and her shriek when my car jumped the curb. Her seat, the seat I had forgotten to strap in, flew forward and hit the dash.

I'd been drinking. It's shameful to admit even in my head but it's the truth. I drank, I smoked, and then I got into a car with my beautiful little girl. She was okay, thank God, but nobody else was.

I looked up and met Mary's eyes. Mine were filled with tears and I was shaking as I held my baby. I whispered into her hair, "I'm sorry. I'm so sorry." In that moment, looking into my wife's eyes over the heads of our children, I knew she was seeing not only the car accident that could have been so much worse, but everything I'd ever done to hurt her or the children—the affairs, the bounced checks, the stealing, the hiding, the yelling...my face burned with shame and hot tears dripped down my cheeks.

With everything I had, I tried to make Mary see just how sorry I was for everything. *It wasn't me*, I pleaded silently. *None of it was me.*

The problem was, it *was* me. All of it. The alcohol may have made me do it, but I chose to drink. I set my chin on my daughter's head with a shaky sigh.

My wife just smiled sadly.

It's much too early to think about forgiveness.

The incident shook me, but it was a reminder of who I'm doing this for. It's only been a few days, but I think I can do it this time. I *want* to do it. I want to get back to being *me*, whoever that is. I think that will be the hardest part in all of this. Just being myself. Accepting all my faults just as they are, recognizing my strengths … if I have any.

But first, I just need to get back to being human. How do people do that without drinking?

8:00 p.m.

When everyone left the facility and I was alone again in my chair, I felt depressed. Lost.

Most of my days here, I cnd up feeling lost.

I think I've felt that way most of my life.

Happy Birthday to me.

The Last Mermaid

The first time I saw her was after the Purge. It should have been impossible. She was supposed to be dead. And she nearly was.

I almost didn't notice her. I'd been so lost in self-pity, she almost died right there next to me. I was sitting on the edge of the water, my scuba gear spread out beside me, considering just throwing it all into the ocean and walking away. The thrill of the job, diving, observing and recording aquatic life, things that no one else got to see, was now gone. The peace I found reaching depths that few on land ever got to experience, evaporated the moment I put a price tag on it.

It was the sudden splash that attracted my attention. The splash that, looking back, I was surprised she even had the strength to make. I'd turned toward the noise and there she was. Her teal tail was wrapped in the thick twine of the hunter's nets, streaks of blood flowing down onto the sand, and the glowing skin I'd observed on so many of her kind was dull and pallid. But she was, impossibly, alive. The last of her kind. The last mermaid.

I'd spent years watching them, recording their patterns, their habits, their lifestyles, and now the last one was about to die beside me. It seemed almost fitting, given the part I had played in their destruction.

But she didn't die.

It took weeks of nursing her back to health, but when her wounds had almost healed, she looked up at me from the shore just outside my beachside shack.

"How can I repay you?"

I refused to meet her sparkling, emerald eyes. Weeks of caring for her and I hadn't once made eye contact.

"You don't. You go hide and do not come to the surface. Ever."

She didn't argue. Her head dropped and she pushed away from me. My hand, that had been removing the last of her bandages, slid down the smooth length of the scales of her tail until it rested on air. I watched her disappear into the waves.

I didn't see her after that, but I often sensed her presence. When I was diving, rediscovering my love for the ocean I'd exposed for profit, I felt her, just out of sight. At night, she hovered right off shore and knowing she was there comforted me, a comfort I didn't deserve.

I took to sleeping in my hammock on the shore so I could hear her splash to the surface every night and spread out on the beach beside me. I assumed she was lonely, like me. And sad, but for different reasons. Her family was gone; mine, just out of reach. We were kindred spirits in a way, my actions the cause of our grief. We didn't talk, didn't interact, we simply lived side by side in peaceful sorrow. Until Alexa Winters called.

***

"Rich Easter! Our local, yet elusive, celebrity." I shivered at the label and she noticed.

"You don't like the term?" She stepped back, motioning for me to come inside. "Your research was integral in the capturing…"

"Yes." I was well aware of the implications of my research. My daughter's hatred of what I had done, her absence and my solitary lifestyle were proof of that. "Though that was never the original intention of my work."

The door swung shut behind me as I stepped into a massive front hall bathed in tile. Ms. Winters and her family funded everything in the city, from the hospitals to the universities to the TV Stations. Their home showed it.

"Well, useful nonetheless," she said as she lit a cigarette. Smoke surrounded her dark hair and sharp, angled face. "Mr. Easter, I have something to show you."

I followed her through the bowels of the Winter estate. The twisting turns and long hallways eventually led to a plain, white door with a hefty padlock. She didn't say anything as she used one hand to spin the combination and the other to hold her cigarette. When the door opened, she wordlessly started down a set of stairs and I followed her trail of smoke. When she stopped, it appeared we'd reached a rotunda.

"I don't show many people what I am about to show you, Mr. Easter." She turned, running her hand along the wall until there was a click and the room in front of us was flooded with light. I squinted against the sudden brightness and my stomach flipped as I took in the room. Cages lined the walls of the round chamber. Ms. Winters gave me a nudge, urging me farther into the room.

It was like the Purge all over again. The Purge that I'd helped begin.

In the dark days after the declaration that all creatures not of human descent should be rounded up and destroyed, cages just like these lined the streets. The public hurried past them, lowering their eyes because it was too gut-wrenching to see the creatures—that often looked human—cowering or howling for their families. But they'd been told it was for the best. Science showed the creatures had dirty genes and top officials said they were dangerous. Even Alexa Winters agreed. Especially after the wereboy attacked and killed her only son.

Now, looking around this room, this twisted version of Noah's Ark, I felt that same twist of guilt in my stomach I'd felt during and after the Purge.

The werewolf in the cage to my immediate right sighed deeply and leaned back against the wall from his sitting position on the floor. He was in human form but I knew he was a wolf-man because of the sign attached to the front of his cage. There were other signs, too.

Vampire.

Fairy.

Shapeshifter.

Gnome.

I vaguely wondered why they didn't use their power and strength to simply break out. Then, I saw the gun. Perched outside of the werewolf cage, it was aimed inside and a long piece of wire led from each of the bars of the cage, to the trigger. I assumed the bullets were silver. My eyes fell to the vampire's cage, laced in garlic, in which sat a young girl, barely sixteen.

"Its potency has been increased," she said, coming up behind me. "The real stuff just burns them a little. This will eat her skin like battery acid."

I stared at her as she looked around the room proudly.

"Besides," she added, tossing her cigarette onto the cement floor and stomping it out. "They don't have any reason to escape. They're the last of their kind. The very last. No families. No partners to mate with and spread their filthy genes through our world again. We let them get out of control once. It won't happen again."

"But…" I tried to whisper around the bile forming in my throat, "Why not just kill them? Why…" I motioned around the room, *"this?"*

She shrugged. "Call it a hobby. Something just for me. They took something from me I'll never get back. I'm returning the favor."

"Why are you showing me this?" I whispered, though I already had an idea. In my head, I saw a flash of green tail, heard the familiar splash that signaled her appearance.

Ms. Winters lifted her hand to just below her chin and wiggled her slender finger toward the center of the room.

I turned. I'd been so distracted by the cages I hadn't even noticed the empty display in the middle of the room: a large pool with a rock in the middle. My stomach rolled.

"I have a job for you."

"But … they're gone." I tried to keep my voice steady around my lie. "They were all caught in the round up."

She smiled a knowing smile. "You know as well as I do that's not true."

How did she know?

"Well, I don't want your money."

"I thought you might say that. So, I've added … *incentive*. I know your daughter's schedule, her school address. I know your ex-wife's

70

address, and I know people who will do anything for a buck. You're familiar with those people, Mr. Easter. You used to be one."

I shook my head, "You can't do that. I'll report you. I'll tell the papers, the police."

She laughed. "I own the papers *and* the police. Who do you think funded the paycheck that bought your research? I own this city. You can't fight me."

***

"Please, come out!" I called from the beach, knowing she wouldn't be far. "It's okay, I know you're there. I need to talk to you."

She surfaced sheepishly a few feet from the shore. The waves carried her up to me and she settled onto the sand, her mossy, dark hair falling across her bare chest, her tail tucked under her.

I stood in front of her, towering over her but feeling small.

"I have a problem."

She reached up and took my hand. How was hers so warm? "Tell me."

I told her everything, from the moment I walked into Alexa Winters' home to her impossible request and her threats to my daughter.

"I came here to catch you. To take you to her." Suddenly my legs would no longer support me. I fell to my knees in front of her and grabbed her shoulders, meeting her eyes for the first time since I'd known her.

They sparkled like the sun on the water and it was like the first time I dove into the ocean alone — peaceful and exhilarating at the same time.

"But, I can't…" I whispered. "I can't do it."

I felt her body relax under my grip and she sighed, bringing her hands to either side of my face. "You will."

"What? But ... you're the last of your kind. If…"

She cut me off. "Yes, I am. But you are not the last of yours. You have a family, a daughter that needs you."

"No." It's a guttural noise more than a word. "Don't you know who I am? What I've done to you?"

"You saved…"

"I killed you all. It was *my* research that helped them hunt you down, my observations of your family and your people ... it was my work that sentenced you all to death. I sold it. I profited off your extinction."

Her hands were still on my face, mine still on her shoulders, but she pulled her gaze from mine and her hair fell down like a curtain.

"I don't deserve your help," I told her.

She lifted her head again, her eyes meeting mine but no longer sparkling. They were dark and stormy and determined. "It doesn't matter. Your daughter does not deserve to suffer for your mistakes. You sentenced me to a life alone. Let me have this final act of kindness."

***

The last time I saw her, she was drifting into the net attached to one of Alexa Winters' boats. She'd lifted one hand, slowly, sadly, before disappearing under the surface. The boat would drag the net to the canal that ran behind the estate and from there she would be transferred to her new home as the prize piece in the collection of Alexa Winters.

I was informed by Ms. Winters, after I was assured my daughter was safe and my payment was deposited, that the collection would soon be moved to a new, unknown location. Obviously, she didn't trust me. I would have to move fast.

I threw a crowbar, a blow torch, my diving knife and a gun into my dive bag. My ex was already on her way out of the country with Molly and I'd transferred my entire payment into her account.

I secured my dive mask and broke the surface of the waves, the ocean welcoming me home. I could swim to the canals and from there find a way into the estate's basement. If I couldn't, I would make one. As soon as the weapons were cleared from the room, the others would be able to help me. They would all be free and the last mermaid would not die on display. I may have put her there, but I would not leave her there.

The Problem with Humans

"When was the last time you saw her?"

"Was she happy at home?"

"Could she have run away?"

The kid working at the coffee shop was trying to play detective but mostly he was getting on Anton's nerves.

"Look, kid. I just need to know if you've seen her. The GPS on my tracking app showed this as her last location."

"Tracking app? That's not cool, man."

"I'm not trying to be cool. I'm trying to find my daughter."

The truth was, he'd never had to use it before. Arabelle was a teenager, but she was a good kid. She knew the rules—if you're not going to be home for dinner, check in—and she followed them. Except for tonight. She hadn't come home for dinner and she hadn't called.

He was probably worried over nothing, but with things the way they were right now, it was too dangerous for her to be out past dark. The tracking app, the one she'd consented to if he only used it in an emergency, had shown her here, at the coffee shop where she liked to do homework.

Actually, it had taken him to the sidewalk outside. When he'd come inside, the only person in the trendy shop with its light wood and sharp angles was the kid.

"Hey. I told you, man. My shift just started and the last guy is gone. You're my first customer of the day. You gonna buy anything or not?"

Anton raised his eyebrows at the scrawny teenager. Human kids were the worst. How dare this punk ask if his daughter was happy. Of course she was happy. She didn't know what it was like to hide in the darkness; her life had been spent in the light. The slow adaptation of their species to daylight, over millions of years, meant that they'd eventually had to find ways to survive among the living. When the humans decided they were enlightened enough to welcome vampires and other Supernaturals into their world, they'd been able to come out of hiding for the first time in...well, ever. It was the only life Arabelle had ever known.

The TV behind the counter blared the latest news, *"Human, non-human tensions continue to rise after a wereboy attacked the son of philanthropist Alexa Winters. After thirty-five years of peace, humans now say they fear for their lives around their supernatural co-workers, neighbors, and friends as riots, protests, and rallies erupt across the country."*

At the anchor's announcement, the boy eyed Anton's pale skin suspiciously, glancing up to his mouth. While Anton usually didn't

76

usually condone intimidation, he grinned, showing off his fangs. The kid took a step back.

To add a little urgency to the kid's answer, Anton poked at the cactus next to the cash register, piercing his bare finger. No blood. No pain. "I said, *have you seen her?*"

The kid winced. "Sorry, sir. I haven't seen her. Maybe call the police?"

Anton scoffed. "Yeah, that's gonna go well right now."

It may have been a werekid that attacked that boy, but ever since then, every Supernatural was the same. Savage. Unable to control their urges or their young. It didn't matter that most of them had been around longer than most humans alive today—they were only safe as long as they followed the human's rules. And they hadn't. Someone's kid had broken the trucc and now tensions were high—too high for a sixteen-year-old non-human to be out on her own. People were scared and their fear was aimed at anyone who was different, whether or not they were actually a threat.

In his hand, Anton's phone went dark. He looked down and saw the app had lost its connection to Arabelle's phone. Not good.

He left the kid behind the register and rushed outside. A truck was pulling forward as another one pulled up to replace it. The back of the new truck opened and if Anton had a beating heart, it would have stopped. The truck was filled with cages.

"What the hell…?"

Still no signal from the phone, but it had gone out right around here. Before he could decide his next move, his phone beeped again, this time with the national alert system. Looking around, Anton caught a glimpse of a TV in a nearby bar.

On the screen, an empty podium waited. There were dozens of microphones but no press. Whoever was about to speak wanted the whole world to see but didn't want anyone else in the room with them. The news ticker at the bottom of the screen displayed a scrolling bad omen for every non-human.

"Son of philanthropist Alexa Winters, hospitalized since an attack by a wereboy, has died from his injuries."

Shit. This changed everything. Alexa Winters was a big deal. There was nothing in this city, probably the state, she didn't have her hands, and her money, in. They might have stood a chance with the courts if the kid had lived, but with the death of the boy ... well, things were not going to go their way.

From behind a velvet curtain a woman with her head bowed, clad all in black, approached the podium. Alexa Winters lifted her gaze to the cameras and began to speak.

"The creatures we once welcomed into our society have not honored their end of the Peace Accords. For generations, we lived peacefully together. Not anymore. The creature who took my son from me has been put down. The Accords stated there would be a zero-tolerance policy when it came to attacks on humans. We *must* enforce that policy."

The ticker changed.

"After months of deliberation, the courts rules in favor of Alexa Winters. All supernatural creatures to be exterminated."

"Friends, I've heard your cries. I've felt your fear. From my son's deathbed I watched you all march for the right to be safe in your own world. I read your signs, I received your letters of sympathy and desperation. You've been searching for an answer. With the death of my son, it has begun," she continued. "As I speak, these creatures are being rounded up. They will be transferred to secure facilities and exterminated. Not just werewolves. Mermaids, biters, all non-humans nationwide will be eliminated."

Eliminated. Anton looked desperately around but he knew no one would come forward to help them. The "peace" they'd been living in was a ruse. When it came down to it, it was humans above anyone else and it always would be. The only thing he cared about now was finding his daughter. With no reason to maintain a pretense of peace, he took a breath and bellowed, "Arabelle!"

From the truck in front of him, he heard it. A whimper. A call. He rushed forward and yanked up on the door of the truck.

"Arabelle!"

"Daddy!" she sobbed. Then her eyes widened. "Dad, look out!"

A Warm Welcome

"Wha...what happened?" I mumble, fighting whatever sedative was in the needle that had managed to puncture my skin. *Musta been pure silver,* I think groggily. I fight the buzzing in my head to pull myself into a sitting position but immediately fall back down. *Fucking strong sedative.* I struggle to remember the events that put me here.

I'd already made coffee (yes, werewolves drink coffee, you specist prick) and the 9:00 news was on. That philanthropist's kid, the one who'd been attacked by a wereboy, had just died. The attack happened a few months ago and me and the other Supernaturals had been hoping things would calm down as the kid healed...guess not. His death wasn't good for any of us. I hadn't waited around to find out just how not good it was. Instead, I headed out to grab the mail.

I don't think I even made it to my mailbox. There were a shit ton of trucks up and down my street and ... I think I remember a scream? And turning toward it? Then ... nothing. Some sunnavabitch musta snuck up behind me. Takes alotta nerve to sneak up behind a hairy mother like me still in their bathrobe. I guess the "peaceful coexistence" we were promised by the humans all those years ago is over.

Outlining the edge of the circular room I now find myself in are simple black cages. Cages like the one I'm in right now. One I might not be getting out of anytime soon, I begin to realize. Most are empty but one holds an unconscious young woman, species unclear, crumbled on the floor.

"That garlic elixir was a little stronger than I intended." I jump at the voice just outside my cage and my eyes struggle to focus on the form. It's oddly familiar. "She'll wake up soon, though," she continues and I realize how I know her. She was on the news every few days, dedicating buildings, opening new foundations, and most recently because of her son...

Alexa Winters: rich bitch and mother of the boy that had just died. She was grinning from ear to ear.

Suddenly I wonder if I'm grateful I woke up or wishing I hadn't.

"This some sort of perverted zoo?" I mumble.

She laughs. "Close." She flips a switch that illuminates signs on the front of each cage. The unconscious girl's sign says, "Vampire." There's an empty "Shape Shifter," and beside me, glowing neon in the dark basement, "Werewolf."

I push myself to the back corner of my cage as it slides into place beside the sign. She holds her arms out wide and grins. "Welcome," she gives a half spin, "to my collection."

About Allison Spooner

Allison Spooner writes short fiction because she loves the challenge of bringing worlds, characters, and stories to life in as few words as possible. This is her second collection of short fiction. You can find more of her stories in, "Flash in the Dark: A Collection of Flash Fiction. She offers workshops and talks on using flash fiction to flash your muse and get writing. You can read more of her work on her website, www.allisonspoonerwriter.com.

Like what you read? Spread the word, leave a review.

Made in the USA
Monee, IL
08 August 2021